I AM READING

DOUGHNUT DANGER

ANTHONY MASTERS

ILLUSTRATED BY
CHRIS FISHER

KINGFISHER
BOSTON

For Cathy and Tom Maskery with love—A. M.

KINGFISHER
a Houghton Mifflin Company imprint
222 Berkeley Street
Boston, Massachusetts 02116
www.houghtonmifflinbooks.com

First published by Kingfisher in 2003
This edition published in 2004
2 4 6 8 10 9 7 5 3 1
1TR/0604/AJT/GRS(GRS)/115SMA

LIBRARY OF CONGRESS CATALOGING–IN–PUBLICATION DATA
has been applied for.

ISBN 0-7534-5821-7

Printed in India

Contents

Chapter One
The Rats Are Back
4

Chapter Two
The Rats' Hideout
9

Chapter Three
The Missing Mouse
18

Chapter Four
Max Has a Plan
27

Chapter Five
A Sticky End
35

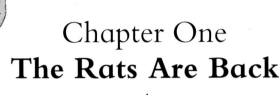

Chapter One
The Rats Are Back

Max Mouse was opening a package of plain doughnuts.

Mel and Molly were helping him.

"At last," said Max as the package split open. "This is the moment we've been waiting for!"

"Yummy," said Mel, biting into a doughnut.

"Delicious," squeaked Molly as she took a nibble.

Suddenly Max stopped eating.

"Did you see that?" hissed Max.

"What?" whispered Molly.

"I thought I saw a rat's tail."

The three mice looked at each other.
The rats were gangsters. The mice had
had trouble with them before.
Then they heard a horrible sound.
"I know that laugh," Max whispered.
"So do I," said Mel. "That's Ricky Rat."

The laughter was coming from the basement.
The basement door was half open. There
was a message pinned next to the door:

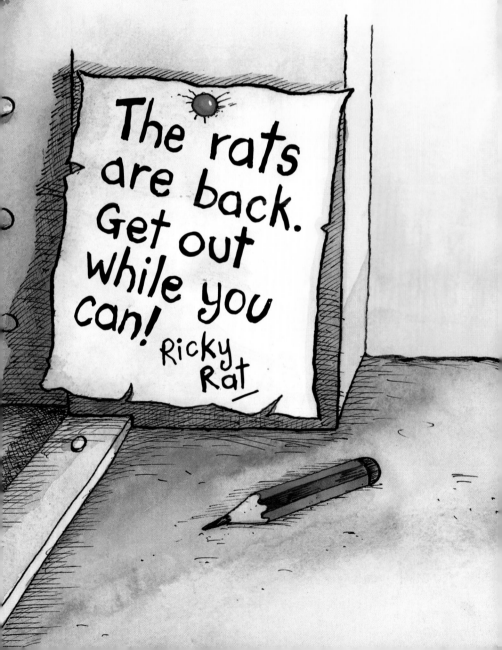

"What are we going to do?" asked Mel.

"We've only just moved into this

doughnut factory," said Molly with a sigh.

"And no one's moving us out," said Max.

"Not even Ricky Rat."

Chapter Two
The Rats' Hideout

"We'll have to get rid of the rats," said Max. "Let's take a look at their hideout and see what they're up to down there." The mice crept past the doughnut-making machine.

Mel looked up at it nervously.

The machine was scary in the dark.

10

The mice got to the basement door.

It was still half open, and they could

see a light.

"Be careful. This could be a trap,"

whispered Molly.

"Come on," said Max.

The mice crept down the basement stairs.

They stopped at the bottom and looked

into the basement.

Max didn't like what he saw.

Mel and Molly didn't like

what they saw either.

There was one electric lightbulb
hanging over a pool table.
The rat gang was playing a game.

"My shot," said Ricky.

He pushed Ronnie Rat out of the way with his pool cue.

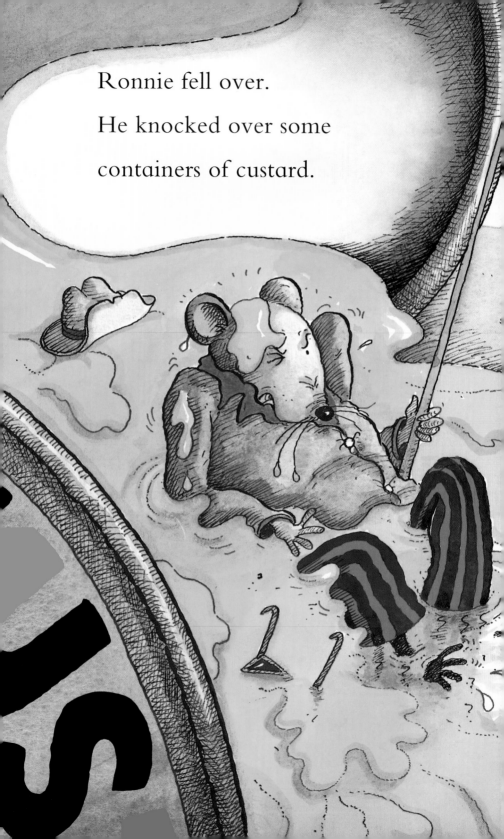

Ronnie fell over.

He knocked over some

containers of custard.

Custard spilled all over the floor
and all over Ronnie.

The rest of the rat gang laughed.

"Let's get out of here!" said Max.

He quickly ran up the stairs.

Molly was close behind him.

Mel turned around to follow.

But he slipped on some custard

and slid right under the pool table.

"Looks like we've got mice,"

sneered Ronnie.

"You're right, Ronnie," said Ricky.

"And we know how to deal with mice!"

Chapter Three
The Missing Mouse

Max and Molly ran out of the basement

and hid behind some bags of sugar.

"Where's Mel?" asked Molly.

"I thought he was behind you," said Max.

"He must still be in the basement."

Max and Molly were afraid.
But they had to find Mel.
They crept down the
basement stairs again.

"No," squeaked Molly.
"I don't believe it."

19

Mel was wearing a blindfold.

The rats had put a broom handle

over a big vat of jam.

They were making Mel walk the plank!

Ronnie was standing on a pile of boxes

next to the vat.

"Start walking!" he ordered.

21

 "What are we
going to do?"
whispered Molly.
"I'm going to rescue Mel," said Max.
There were some shelves behind the
vat of jam. Max ran over to them.
So far none of the rats had seen him.

THIS WAY
UP

THIS WAY
UP

Max climbed up onto
the shelves.
"There's another mouse!"
Ronnie shouted, jumping
down from the boxes.
"Get him!" yelled Ricky.
But Max was too fast.

Max jumped onto the broom handle.

Mel was too frightened to move.

Max pulled off Mel's blindfold.

"Quick!" he shouted as he pulled Mel

onto the edge of the vat. "Jump!"

The two mice jumped down and raced

across the floor.

Ronnie tried to jump too, but he lost

his balance and fell into the vat of jam.

"Help!" Ronnie shouted as he splashed around in the jam.

The rats stared over the edge of the vat.

"You idiot!" said Ricky.

He turned to the other rats.

"Get Ronnie out of there!" he shouted.

"Then follow me. We're going to get those mice!"

Chapter Four
Max Has a Plan

Max, Mel, and Molly met up behind
a big bag of flour.

"That was close," gasped Molly.

"We need to get rid of those rats,"
said Max. "And I think I know just
how we can do that."

He began to whisper to Molly and Mel.

The rats were looking for the mice.
Ronnie was making squeaking sounds as
he walked. He was still covered in jam.

Max jumped out from behind the bag
of flour.

"Come and get me!" he squeaked.

"Don't worry," hissed Ricky. "We'll
get you all right."

29

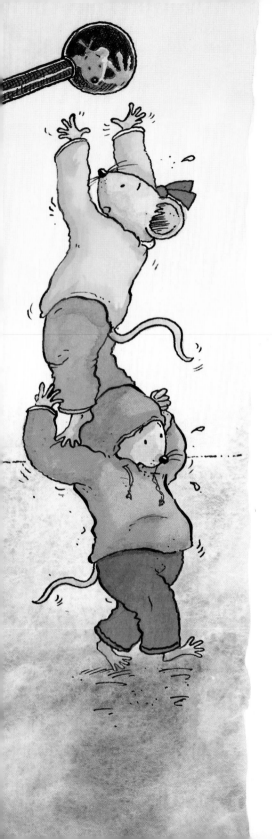

While the rats were chasing Max, Mel and Molly tiptoed under the doughnut-making machine.

"Bend down so I can get up on your shoulders," whispered Molly. Mel began to wobble.

"You're too heavy," he squeaked.

"I can't hold you."

"If I can just reach the switch," said Molly, "I can get the conveyor belt moving. Then Max can take those rats for a ride."

But Mel was really wobbling now. The two mice ended up in a pile on the floor.

Max was running in circles.

He was getting very tired.

Ricky and his rat gang were starting

to catch up with him.

Max felt a nasty nip on his tail

several times.

What are Mel and Molly doing, he

wondered. *Why don't they hurry up?*

Molly climbed onto Mel's
shoulders again.
Mel tried hard not to wobble.
Molly reached up
toward the switch.
"I can't hold on
much longer,"
Mel gasped.
"Almost got it,"
said Molly as she
reached up higher.

At last there was a click as she pulled the switch down.

The machine made a loud clanking sound and started making doughnuts.

Chapter Five
A Sticky End

The conveyor belt was moving.

Max jumped onto it.

Ricky and the rat gang were close
behind him.

Freshly made doughnuts were coming
out of the machine.

The doughnuts were heading
toward the packing machine.
So were Max and the rat gang.
Max ran as fast as he could along
the conveyor belt, dodging between
the doughnuts.

The machine began to shower
the doughnuts with sugar.
Max dodged the sugar.
So did the rats.

Then the machine began to squirt

frosting on the doughnuts.

Max dodged the frosting.

But Ronnie got splattered.

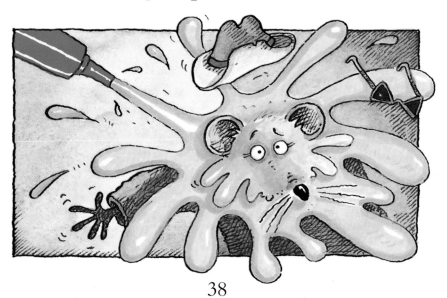

Suddenly the machine was squirting
chocolate.

Max dodged again.

But Ricky was too slow. He got splashed.

Max was way out
in front now.
He could see the
mechanical arms
of the doughnut-
packing machine.
They were
grabbing the
doughnuts and
putting them
into boxes.

DOUGHN

Max got ready to jump off.

"Now!" he yelled.

Molly and Mel ran under the machine

and held up a sheet of plastic wrap.

"Here I come!" shouted Max.

He jumped and landed safely on the

plastic wrap.

"Watch out!" yelled Ricky to the
rat gang.
But it was too late.

Max, Molly, and Mel were sitting
on top of the packing machine,
nibbling doughnuts.

They watched as boxes of doughnuts
moved along the conveyor belt.

"There they go," said Mel, staring
down at one of the boxes.

Inside each doughnut was a rat.

"They don't look too happy," said Max.

"Bye, bye," squeaked Molly as the
conveyor belt took the box out of the
factory. Soon it would be loaded onto
a van and taken to the supermarket.

"Those doughnuts are going to be a real surprise," said Mel, licking sugar off his whiskers.

"You bet they are," laughed Max. "They're the first rat-flavored doughnuts ever made!"

About the author and illustrator

Anthony Masters used to run a children's theater and also taught drama and writing courses in schools and libraries. But he is best known for his own stories for children.
He says, "Rats make brilliant baddies, and the rats in this story are always up to no good.
I think Max Mouse and his friends are really brave to stand up against Ricky and his gang."

Chris Fisher's favorite subject at school was art, and now he is the illustrator of more than 70 books for children. Chris enjoyed inventing all the exciting machines for the mice's doughnut factory home. He says, "I would love to live in a doughnut factory. But I would never get any work done. I would spend all day munching jam doughnuts. Yummy!"

Strategies for Independent Readers

Predict
Think about the cover, illustrations, and the title of the book. What do you think this book will be about? While you are reading think about what may happen next and why.

Monitor
As you read ask yourself if what you're reading makes sense. If it doesn't, reread, look at the illustrations, or read ahead.

Question
Ask yourself questions about important ideas in the story such as what the characters might do or what you might learn.

Phonics
If there is a word that you do not know, look carefully at the letters, sounds, and word parts that you do know. Blend the sounds to read the word. Ask yourself if this is a word you know. Does it make sense in the sentence?

Summarize
Think about the characters, the setting where the story takes place, and the problem the characters faced in the story. Tell the important ideas in the beginning, middle, and end of the story.

Evaluate
Ask yourself questions like: Did you like the story? Why or why not? How did the author make the story come alive? How did the author make the story fun to read? How well did you understand the story? Maybe you can understand it better if you read it again!